Put Beginning Readers on the Right Track with
ALL ABOARD READING™

The All Aboard Reading series is especially designed for beginning readers. Written by noted authors and illustrated in full color, these are books that children really want to read—books to excite their imagination, expand their interests, make them laugh, and support their feelings. With fiction and nonfiction stories that are high interest and curriculum-related, All Aboard Reading books offer something for every young reader. And with four different reading levels, the All Aboard Reading series lets you choose which books are most appropriate for your children and their growing abilities.

Picture Readers
Picture Readers have super-simple texts, with many nouns appearing as rebus pictures. At the end of each book are 24 flash cards—on one side is a rebus picture; on the other side is the written-out word.

Station Stop 1
Station Stop 1 books are best for children who have just begun to read. Simple words and big type make these early reading experiences more comfortable. Picture clues help children to figure out the words on the page. Lots of repetition throughout the text helps children to predict the next word or phrase—an essential step in developing word recognition.

Station Stop 2
Station Stop 2 books are written specifically for children who are reading with help. Short sentences make it easier for early readers to understand what they are reading. Simple plots and simple dialogue help children with reading comprehension.

Station Stop 3
Station Stop 3 books are perfect for children who are reading alone. With longer text and harder words, these books appeal to children who have mastered basic reading skills. More complex stories captivate children who are ready for more challenging books.

In addition to All Aboard Reading books, look for All Aboard Math Readers™ (fiction stories that teach math concepts children are learning in school); All Aboard Science Readers™ (nonfiction books that explore the most fascinating science topics in age-appropriate language); and All Aboard Poetry Readers™ (funny, rhyming poems for readers of all levels).

All Aboard for happy reading!

GROSSET & DUNLAP
Published by the Penguin Group
Penguin Group (USA) Inc., 375 Hudson Street, New York, New York 10014, USA
Penguin Group (Canada), 90 Eglinton Avenue East, Suite 700, Toronto,
Ontario M4P 2Y3, Canada (a division of Pearson Penguin Canada Inc.)
Penguin Books Ltd., 80 Strand, London WC2R 0RL, England
Penguin Group Ireland, 25 St. Stephen's Green, Dublin 2, Ireland
(a division of Penguin Books Ltd.)
Penguin Group (Australia), 250 Camberwell Road, Camberwell, Victoria 3124,
Australia (a division of Pearson Australia Group Pty. Ltd.)
Penguin Books India Pvt. Ltd., 11 Community Centre, Panchsheel Park,
New Delhi—110 017, India
Penguin Group (NZ), 67 Apollo Drive, Rosedale, North Shore 0632, New Zealand
(a division of Pearson New Zealand Ltd.)
Penguin Books (South Africa) (Pty.) Ltd., 24 Sturdee Avenue,
Rosebank, Johannesburg 2196, South Africa

Penguin Books Ltd., Registered Offices:
80 Strand, London WC2R 0RL, England

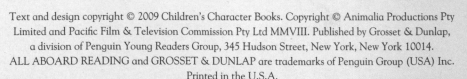

Library of Congress Control Number: 2008043831

ISBN 978-0-448-45196-1   10 9 8 7 6 5 4 3 2 1

ANIMALIA

The Animal Within

By Rachel Rose

Based on the teleplay by Deanna Oliver and Sherri Stoner

Grosset & Dunlap

It was mealtime in Animalia.
Alex and Zoe were sitting at the
Elephant's Eatery.
Suddenly they heard loud, rude noises
coming from a nearby table.

Zoe looked over her shoulder.
She saw Herry and Horble Hog
eating their breakfasts.
The hogs were making a huge mess.
There was food everywhere!

Zoe was shocked by the hogs' bad table manners.
"Excuse me, but could you please chew with your mouths closed?" asked Zoe.

The hogs nodded their heads to say yes.
But two seconds later they were chewing
with their mouths open again!
Zoe pushed her plate to the side.
"I have lost my appetite now," she said.
G'Bubu Gorilla picked up her plate and
started to finish Zoe's food.

Just then, Iggy D'Iguana came over and
hopped onto the table.
"Tonight is the big reenactment
of the signing of the Bill of Writes.
You have memorized your lines, yes?"
he asked Zoe and Alex.

"Yes, Iggy. We know our lines," Zoe said.
Iggy was planning a big party to celebrate
the day when Animalians
learned how to read and write.
Iggy wanted Zoe and Alex
to act out the signing of the Bill of Writes
in his show.

Iggy said the Bill of Writes helped
Animalians become civilized.
Zoe pointed to the hogs as they shoved more
food into their mouths.

"Well, not everyone became civilized,"
she said.
She looked over at Horble.
He was showing Herry his dirty tissue!

The hogs continued to burp, spit,
and make a mess.
Zoe couldn't believe her eyes.
"Can't they learn some manners?" she asked.
"Face it. They're just *animals*," Alex told her.

G'Bubu's eyes widened in surprise.
"What do you mean, *just animals?*" G'Bubu asked.
"We are *all* animals, you included," Iggy said.
"*We'd* never act like hogs," Zoe said as she rolled her eyes.

The hogs heard Alex and Zoe making fun
of them.
It hurt their feelings.
So they went over to talk to Alex and Zoe.
"You shouldn't be making sport of us, actin'
like you're better and such," Herry said.

Alex and Zoe felt bad about hurting the hogs' feelings.
They were about to say sorry when a toucan flew onto the table.
It was the Hoity-Toity Bird.
He was also eating in the restaurant that morning.
He heard what Alex and Zoe said and thought they sounded like snobs.

With a flash of bright light, he cast a spell on Alex and Zoe!

They sat at the table with their mouths
hanging open like apes.
"Ooh ooh, ah ooh!" Alex called.

Iggy tried to talk to Zoe, but she picked him up and sniffed him instead! "Ooh ooh, ah ooh!" Zoe called.

Zoe and Alex crawled along the counter.
They even started to throw cups.
Alex and Zoe hooted, hollered, and screeched.

Iggy was not happy to see such a mess.
"Alex and Zoe cannot perform tonight!"
Iggy called as he dodged a flying spoon.
He was counting on Alex and Zoe
to remember their lines about the Bill of Writes.
But all they could say was, "Ooh ooh, ah ooh!"

"Ain't right to let 'em get left outta the party just 'cuz some bird threw a hex on 'em," Herry said.
Herry rubbed his chin as he thought about what to do.

Even though Alex and Zoe
had made fun of the hogs, Herry and Horble
still wanted to help out.
"'Erry and I'll learn 'em the skit!" Horble said.

"And we'll learn 'em 'ow to talk properlike and be fine, upstanding animals like we hogs," Herry said as he grabbed Zoe's hand.

Back at the hogs' workshop, Herry
and Horble began their lessons.
"The word for food is *grub*," said Herry.
Alex and Zoe growled and grunted back
at the hogs.

Suddenly, Herry let out a loud burp.
The kids copied him and let out
two huge burps!
They were not off to a good start.

Next, the hogs tried to teach the kids
how to speak in full sentences.
But the hogs' sentences didn't make any sense!
"'At's a beauty, innit?" said Herry.
"A booty, in it," copied Zoe.
"Attaway, jungle bug!" Horble called out.

Then it was Alex's turn to repeat the sentence. All he could do was say, "A-blah, blah, blah." And then he let out a huge burp!

"What if, at the fancy party, you make a boo-boo or a social fox paw," began Herry. "You bow and say to the offended party: Pardon me, yer maggot-stry," added Horble. (He was trying to say, "Pardon me, your majesty.")

"Pudg-pen ma-yer maggog-grie!"
said Alex as he bowed.
Alex and Zoe were all mixed up.
They would never be ready for
Iggy's show at this rate!

The hogs refused to give up.
They wanted to teach Alex and
Zoe some table manners.
Horble picked up a soup spoon.
"Hold the spoon like this, with
your pinkie finger out like it's
broken in two places," he said.

Alex and Zoe copied him perfectly.
"Scoop soup with spoon," Herry added.
Alex and Zoe copied the hogs.
They made loud slurping noises.

"If you miss your mouth and the spoon goes up your nose, turn away from the table, place your finger next to your nose, and blow!" shouted Horble.

Alex and Zoe copied Horble's example.
The hogs loved it!
"We've got 'em almost as civilized as
us," said Herry.

It was almost time for the show and the hogs still had work to do.
They needed to teach the kids the lines they were going to perform.

But Alex and Zoe were being rude and
would not pay attention.
Alex and Zoe even fell asleep
right in the middle of Herry and
Horble's lesson.

A crowd gathered in the Great Library.
Everyone was excited for the show.
Allegra sang a song about the
Bill of Writes.
The crowd cheered for her.

Then Alex and Zoe walked in
with the hogs.
"Do they know their lines for the
reenactment?
Please tell me yes!" Iggy cried.
"Yes, we learned it to 'em good,"
replied Herry.

Then Alex and Zoe greeted
Livingstone T. Lion, the ruler of Animalia.
"Hoo-hog," they said as they bowed.
Livingstone looked confused.

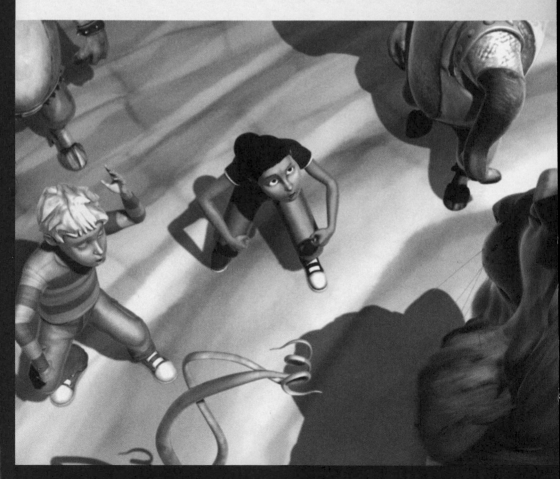

Iggy walked onto the stage.
"And now, the centerpiece of
tonight's festivities, the reenactment
of the signing of the Bill of Writes!"
called Iggy.

Alex and Zoe began their performance.
But instead of saying the lines they
had learned, they acted it out.
Alex and Zoe acted just like the hogs:
They made noises with their armpits,
they waved their arms in the air,
and they shook their behinds.

The crowd did not understand
what was happening onstage.
The Animalians stared at Alex
and Zoe with blank faces.

Iggy began to panic.
This was not what he had planned!
Alex and Zoe continued.
"Ooga-booga-booga," Alex and Zoe
called out.
Then they grabbed a pen and pretended
to sign the Bill of Writes.

"Bill of Writes. Done," said Alex.

"Sign?" asked Zoe.

"Sign," replied Alex.

Zoe pretended to sign her name on the Bill of Writes.

"The end," Alex and Zoe said together.

The crowd was still surprised.
But Livingstone began to clap for
Alex and Zoe.
"Bravo!" he called out.

The crowd quickly caught on and
copied Livingstone.
They clapped and cheered.
Iggy was confused but he walked
onstage to join Alex and Zoe.

"The reenactment was a perfect display
of how far Animalians have come,"
said Livingstone.
"We were all once untamed like
Zoe and Alex just showed us."

Alex and Zoe hugged the hogs.
The Hoity-Toity Bird watched all of
this from the side.
He saw that Alex and Zoe did not think
they were better than everyone.
He saw that the kids loved the hogs.
So he decided to reverse his spell!

"Sorry we made fun of you," Alex said to the hogs.

"Our work 'ere is done," Herry said with a smile.

"Heido-hoo-hog and away!" the hogs called as they ran out of the library.